DATE DUE

Imagine A Dragon

Laurence Pringle • Illustrated by Eujin Kim Neilan

BOYDS MILLS PRESS
HONESDALE, PENNSYLVANIA

To my sisters, Marleah and Linda—
strong, smart women who have slain
more than a few dragons in their lives
—L.P.

Boyds Mills Press, Inc.
815 Church Street
Honesdale, Pennsylvania 18431
Printed in China

Library of Congress Cataloging-in-Publication Data

Pringle, Laurence P.
  Imagine a dragon / Laurence Pringle ; illustrated by Eujin Kim Neilan. — 1st ed.
    p. cm.
  ISBN-13: 978-1-56397-328-4 (hardcover : alk. paper)
  1. Dragons—Juvenile literature. I. Neilan, Eujin Kim, ill. II. Title.
  GR830.D7P75 2008
  398.24'54—dc22
                                        2007017575

First edition
The text of this book is set in 14-point Goudy.
The illustrations are done in acrylic.

10 9 8 7 6 5 4 3 2 1

CLOSE YOUR EYES.

IMAGINE YOU ARE IN A CAVE.

You shine a flashlight into the inky darkness. And there, deep inside,
you come face-to-face with a DRAGON!

But what kind of dragon do you see? Is it friendly, or is it a scary monster?
The answer may depend on when and where you lived.

People began telling tales of dragons thousands of years ago. In China, dragon stories may have begun when people found fossils of dinosaurs and wondered what kind of creatures they had been. In Egypt and in Babylonia (in the area now known as Iraq), explorers returning from faraway parts of Africa and Asia told of huge snakes and other reptiles they had seen. When people heard about these big, unfamiliar animals, their imaginations ran wild. They imagined dragons.

    Stories about dragons also may have helped to explain unusual or scary events. In those long-ago times, people understood very little about nature. If a drought ruined farm crops or a disease killed cows or sheep, people wondered what caused these disasters. They were also puzzled and frightened by powerful storms, earthquakes, and fire-spewing volcanoes. Sometimes people blamed natural events such as these on imaginary beasts, such as dragons.

In ancient Egypt, for instance, no one understood why the sun rose and set each day. Now we know that the turning of the earth causes everyone to lose sight of the sun for part of every day. The earth keeps turning, so the sun keeps disappearing in the west and then reappearing in the east.

The ancient Egyptians had another explanation. They believed that each day Apep, the dragon of darkness, tried to destroy Ra, the sun god. According to this legend, Ra appeared in the east each morning and sailed across the sky. After vanishing in the west, he traveled underground to reach the east again. Beneath the earth, Ra was attacked by Apep.

Fortunately Ra was saved by Seth, the Egyptian god of wind and storms. Seth slew the dragon, and at dawn Ra sailed into sight once more. But Apep always came back to life and waited to attack again the next night.

Far to the north, in Norway, the first dragon was named Nidhoggr, which means "Dread Biter." Like Apep, Nidhoggr stayed underground. This dragon gnawed at the roots of a huge, invisible tree called Yggdrasil, which the Norse people believed sustained all life on Earth. The tree was defended by eagles and other creatures, including gods called Norns. The Norns were three sisters who stayed underground near the dragon and repaired the damage it caused. For the people of Norway, this ancient legend offered hope that good would win over evil.

In ancient Greece, on the other hand, people told the story of a good dragon. One day a young boy found a baby dragon. He brought it home to keep as a pet, and it slept on his bed. But his parents didn't want a dragon in their home. The boy's father took the little dragon far away and abandoned it.

Years later, after the boy had grown to be a man, he was traveling alone far from home. Bandits attacked him. Suddenly, a great dragon appeared and chased the bandits away. It was the boy's pet, now fully grown, too.

From legends such as these, belief in dragons spread far and wide. Some dragons, such as the one in the ancient Greek tale, were nice. But in Europe, Africa, and western Asia, people usually told stories of fierce, dangerous dragons. Today these imaginary creatures are called Western dragons.

The Western dragons of Europe and England were blamed for all sorts of troubles—and no wonder: they were monsters. They measured more than a hundred feet from their mouths to the tips of their tails. Some had more than one head. Fire or poisonous gases spewed from their mouths. Some had wings and could fly, though they usually hid in caverns, guarding treasures of gold or jewels.

And most Western dragons were almost unbeatable in battle because the scaly armor that covered their bodies protected them from the swords and lances of men who tried to kill them. According to legend, many men tried to slay dragons and failed. However, people love stories of good winning over evil, so there were also tales of men outfighting or outsmarting a big, bad dragon.

A famous tale tells the story of a terrible dragon that lived in a lake by the city of Silene in northern Africa (in present-day Libya), which was then part of the vast Roman Empire. To keep the dragon away from the city, people fed it two sheep each day. When all the sheep were gone, the dragon began to gobble up people.

The city's leaders became desperate. They put the names of all the children in a large brass urn, and each day the unlucky child whose name was drawn became the dragon's meal. One day, the king's own daughter was chosen. She was led to the lakeshore and tied to a stake where the dragon could find her.

But a Roman soldier named George came riding by just as the dragon rose screaming from the lake. As the dragon reared up on its back legs, ready to pounce, George stabbed his lance into the dragon's belly, where its scales were weakest. Then, with one swing of his sword, he lopped off its huge head.

According to legend, George slew other dragons in Germany and England. In the fourteenth century, he was named the patron saint of England.

Another brave man named John Smith used milk to rid an English town of an evil dragon. In England, people often put out pails of milk for dragons to drink. They thought this would keep the dragons from hunting livestock—and them. Rather than offer the dragon a small amount of milk, though, John Smith left a huge vat of it.

The beast came along and drank all of the milk. The giant meal made the dragon sleepy, so it lay down for a nap. John Smith waited until the dragon was sleeping soundly, then he thrust his sword between some of the dragon's scales. He pushed deep, deep into the dragon's body and killed the evil creature.

The dragons that people in England imagined usually had snakelike bodies and no legs. These slithery dragons were called Wurms or Ormes. The most famous of these creatures was the Lambton Wurm.

One day in the fourteenth century, the story goes, a boy caught a very young dragon while fishing. The glistening black Wurm was no bigger than his thumb, but it put up a tremendous fight. The boy started to take it home but changed his mind. He dropped it into a roadside well.

Years passed, and deep in the well's darkness the Wurm grew and grew. Then one day a two-hundred-foot-long dragon slithered out. It began to kill sheep and cows with its poisonous breath and terrorized the countryside around Lambton Castle. Knights who tried to slay the dragon were squeezed to death by the beast.

 Then young Lord Lambton returned from a faraway war. He had been the boy who tossed the little dragon down the well. Now he felt he must defeat the monster he had helped create.

Lord Lambton put on a special suit of armor that was studded with long, sharp spikes. He armed himself with a sword. He then waded into a river toward a boulder where the great Wurm often rested.

With a mighty splash, the dragon's head rose from the water. Swiftly the Wurm wrapped its body around the young lord. It squeezed tighter and tighter. The spikes on Lord Lambton's armor stabbed the dragon. The river ran red with blood from the dragon's many wounds. The terrible Lambton Wurm was dead.

 People in England and Europe loved to hear stories of dragons killed by brave men. People in Japan, China, and other East Asian countries also liked dragon tales. But their stories—and their dragons—were usually very different from those of the West.

In ancient East Asian legends, the dragons were even more powerful than those in the West. But they usually shared the world peacefully with humans. People imagined them to be wise, helpful, and friendly. Today these dragons are called Eastern dragons.

People in East Asia believed that dragons ruled the water of the world. They controlled the flow of all streams and rivers, the water level in ponds and lakes, and even ocean waves.

One ancient dragon legend tells of a man who was fishing in a deep body of water called Smoky Pond, near the village of Yen-Tang. He caught a white eel and was about to cook it when an old man said, "This is the dragon of the river Siang. You must let it go." But the fisherman would not. The next day the whole village disappeared beneath the floodwaters of the river.

Eastern dragons were also in charge of rainfall. In fact, people said that the clouds in the sky were dragon breaths. (Unlike Western dragons, Eastern dragons never breathed fire.) In winter, Eastern dragons lived underwater in bejeweled palaces. This caused winter to be the dry season in Asia. In the spring, dragons flew up into the sky, causing windy, rainy weather and sometimes floods. They lived among the clouds in the summer sky. And in the fall, flights of dragons returning to their undersea homes sometimes caused hurricanes. All year long, the lives of dragons affected the weather.

Sometimes a dragon failed to do its job properly. It might be late in sending summer rains, or it might allow a river to flood farmers' fields. When such things happened, the people knew what to do. They gathered beside watery places, where dragons lived. Then they banged gongs and made other loud noises in order to waken the dragon.

To get the help of a dragon, people sometimes made an offering of its favorite foods. Eastern dragons liked to eat bamboo, milk, and swallows— small birds that often swoop low over water as they catch flying insects. The only time people had to fear being eaten by a dragon was just after they dined on a meal of swallows. They would be in danger if a dragon smelled swallow meat on their breath! To be safe, people who had eaten swallows were advised to stay away from boats, bridges over rivers, lakeshores, and other watery places.

Since dragons were thought to have great power over the weather, and thus over people's lives, Chinese scholars imagined many details of dragon life. They said that mother dragons laid their eggs near rivers and that the eggs hatched during thunderstorms—split open by lightning.

At first the baby dragons looked like little snakes and lived underwater. They grew very slowly. After five hundred years, they developed the head of a carp and were called *kiao*. Two thousand years passed before their heads were shaped somewhat like camels' heads with horns. Then they were called *kioh-lungs*. In another thousand years, they became *ying-lungs*—dragons with wings—and flew to their summer home in the sky.

    In China it was written that a full-grown dragon had the parts of many different animals: a camel's head, a deer's horns, a rabbit's eyes, a cow's ears, a snake's neck, a clam's belly, a carp's scales, an eagle's claws, and a tiger's paws. Today colorful paper dragons with some of these parts can be seen in parades that celebrate the Chinese New Year, especially when the Year of the Dragon begins. In the Chinese calendar, it occurs every twelve years: 2000, 2012, 2024, and so on. Some people believe that children born in the Year of the Dragon will have long lives of good health and great wealth.

Long ago, dragons seemed very real to some people. Now we know that they are just make-believe. But we do use the name *dragon*: for speedy insects called dragonflies that catch mosquitoes, for two-foot-long Australian lizards known as bearded dragons, and for the world's largest lizards—Komodo dragons.

Komodo dragons live on four small islands in Indonesia. They have long, forked tongues; scaly skin; and sharp claws. They grow to be ten feet long and are strong enough to kill goats, pigs, or even people.

Komodo dragons are fascinating real animals. But they have no wings. They do not breathe fire or cause rain to fall. They will never be as scary as the Western dragons or as powerful as the Eastern dragons that people created in their imaginations long ago.